Epic Elements

Ben Waters

First Printing, 2017

ISBN-13:
978-1548257507

ISBN-10:
1548257508

Creative Writing Workshop
http://www.phylcampbell.com/young-
authors.html

To Jacob and Sadie, my two friends who partnered with me from the very beginning and made the dream of an awesome game—and now a novel—come true.

Also to Josie, who, even though she wasn't there from the very beginning, has been an amazing friend, game-player, and encourager throughout the school year.

CHAPTER I

Ben was walking through a dark forest. The trees' leaves shaded the ground, and his shadow was not visible. But Ben could see a light woven between the trees. He curiously followed the light, his feet crushing the leaves beneath him. But suddenly, without warning, the light disappeared. A shadowy black substance leaked through the trees, engulfing Ben's legs in darkness before rising up to cover his whole body. Just as the substance rose over his head...

RRRRRINNNG!

His alarm clock went off. He forgot not to set it because it was mid-June, when school was out. Next year, he would be going into seventh grade. Ben's heart was pounding, but as soon as he realized it was a dream, he yawned and got out of bed. He slowly walked downstairs. It was quiet. He must have been the first one up, which was rare, since he had a sister and a brother.

Then, Jacob, his brother, who was one year younger than Ben, came down as Ben was pouring his yogurt into a bowl. Jacob didn't seem tired. He was dressed neatly in a light blue shirt and jeans while Ben had just slapped on a yellow t-shirt and some loose gray sweatpants to slump downstairs in.

"I feel like something interesting is going to happen today," said Jacob. "I don't know what, but..."

"But what?" asked Ben, mildly intrigued. "By the way, is Sadie coming down?"

"Yes," Jacob replied, "I just got dressed quicker than she did." Ben, Sadie and Jacob all slept in separate bedrooms, but not that far away from each other.

Ben put some yogurt on the table for Jacob, some for Sadie, and gave himself seconds.

"Thanks," Jacob added.

Next, Sadie came down the steps and sat down next to Jacob, probably as tired, if not more, than Ben. She was one year older than Ben, making her the oldest of the three. She took a spoonful of her yogurt, tasted it, and then spit it out.

"What is it?" Ben asked. "Is it bad?"

"No, there's a slip of paper in my yogurt."

"What? A slip of paper? What does it say?" Ben asked. Then he added, "I didn't put it there."

"Me neither," said Jacob. "Is it a toy or something?"

Ben held up the container of yogurt, and stared at it. "No, nothing like, *'Free random slip of paper in every container!'*"

"It just says numbers," Sadie said. "It says... six-one-three."

"Well, I don't know what that would mean. Throw it away." Ben reached out his hand to

7

take the note from Sadie, but Jacob slapped his hand away.

"Maybe it's a sign," he said, obviously looking for some form of adventure.

By this time, everyone was done with their yogurt. They decided to go outside (with permission from their parents, of course... except they didn't get permission, because they were soundly sleeping in their bedroom upstairs).

"Let's go in that cave," said Jacob.

"There was never a cave here before," Ben said to neither Jacob nor Sadie in particular. "Did someone magically put a cave here? This day is very strange... there couldn't be a random cave in someone's backyard..."

But Jacob was already rushing towards the mysterious cave.

"Jacob!" called Sadie.

"Let's go after him," Ben said. He carefully walked in after Jacob. Sadie followed.

They met up with Jacob at the mouth of a stone corridor with glittering crystals sticking out of the walls, glowing light blue and pink.

Jacob insisted they grab the jewels immediately. "We would be rich!"

Sadie held him back. "Let's keep exploring," she said.

When they got to the end of the glittering hallway, they saw nine raised stones on a huge stone wall. The stones formed a three-by-three array, like a tic-tac-toe board.

"I know what these might be for!" exclaimed Ben, kind of trying to be funny, but also meaning what he said. "These are keys for a secret code. The top left is one, top middle is two, top right is three, middle left is four--you get the idea."

"So where do we get the numbers?" Jacob asked, and even though he was looking for adventure, he didn't seem convinced in Ben's idea.

Ben pretended to think for a minute, but really, he thought he already knew the answer. "The set of numbers Sadie found in her yogurt. Six-one-three. I bet that's the secret code!"

"That idea just might be crazy enough to work," said Jacob. He pushed against the middle right stone. "Guys, it's heavy!" He struggled as he tried to push the stone but, even using all his strength, just managed to push it in a little bit.

Sadie struggled, too, as she pushed back the top left stone.

Then, it was Ben's turn. He reached up to the top right stone and pushed. Jacob wasn't exaggerating. It WAS heavy! He just about managed to push it back. He collapsed onto the cold stone floor in exhaustion.

Still, nothing happened.

Did it work? Ben wondered.

Clearly, Jacob and Sadie were thinking the same thing. They looked at one another and scratched their heads. Sadie started walking away.

But then, they heard a rumble. The wall in front of them parted and revealed a hidden chamber.

CHAPTER II

Now THIS is weird, Ben thought.

The room was dimly lit with torches. There was a large, raised area on the stone floor. One of the things on the raised area was a scroll. The paper was tan, and looked very old; however, it was tied together by a shiny, smooth red ribbon.

Sadie picked up the dusty scroll and unrolled it. "What does this say?"

Ben got up. "Read it," he told her.

Sadie read,

"All the elements you must seek

Are in different areas, forest or creek
Once you find the shard, put it in the gem
Soon, it will get filled to the brim
All the shards are somewhere — above or below
The first, the Fire Shard, is in a volcano."

"A volcano!" Ben said excitedly. "It must be in Mount Zekmo!" Mount Zekmo was a famous volcano that was about twenty minutes away from their home.

Apparently, Sadie was thinking about something other than the volcano. "What gem?" she wondered.

"Probably the ones that are right here," said Jacob, pointing next to the place where the scroll used to be. Neither Ben nor Sadie had noticed anything other than the scroll. "There's also a necklace, a brooch, and a bracelet!"

The gems were hexagon-shaped and shining silver with a pointed end, while the pieces of jewelry were stone-gray like the cave they were in. Jacob took a gem and the necklace. There was a hexagon-shaped indent, about as big as a small apple, on the necklace. It looked like the gem would fit inside, so he put it in.

"I guess I should take one if you are," said Ben, taking the bracelet. Attached to the bracelet was another hexagon-shaped indent. Ben found a gem like the one Jacob put in the necklace and completed the bracelet.

Sadie took the brooch, which not surprisingly, also had an indent, and put the last gem into it.

Once the trio left the cave, they went into their house to pick up some things for safety precautions, and then they carefully walked to Mount Zekmo. It was quite tiring, but twenty minutes later, they were there. They found sharp rocks at the base of the volcano. They had brought some glue and glued the sharp rocks to the fingers of their gloves, which they had brought along. They didn't have any other equipment except for helmets, and knee and elbow pads. They also had several ice packs they kept in their pockets and a rope for tying around their waists.

They looked up to the top of the volcano. They decided they had to climb the outside of it to reach the top of the volcano.

They each tied a portion of the rope to their waists. They thought that if one of them slipped, the other two would be able to prevent that person from falling. Ben thought it was more like, if one person fell, they would all go down.

Ben was first. He hoisted himself up. He wasn't sure how he felt about having to carry two other people who were tied to him. Being tied to people and climbing a volcano is much more difficult than most people might think. He grabbed a ledge and pulled himself up. Then he found another ledge, and another. As he went higher, Jacob and Sadie made their starts up the mountain after him. Ben found a ledge about two-thirds the way up the mountain. He pulled himself up on it, thinking it would be a good place to rest while waiting for Jacob and Sadie to join him.

Sadie pulled herself up next. Jacob followed shortly behind. They weren't at the top yet, but they knew they could make it.

On the ledge, Ben and Jacob switched places. Ben used one hand to hold onto the rope for extra support. With his other hand, Ben dug into the hard, brown rock. They got all the way up, and left a few claw marks sprinkled around the edge of the volcano.

After a short break, they re-tied the rope around themselves, with Sadie at one end and Jacob at the other. They were going to go down into the volcano using the inner sides. This time, Sadie went first. "I can't believe we're actually doing this," she spoke. "I'd never think kids our age would climb up and into a volcano."

There were many more ledges around the inside of the volcano, along with pieces of rubble floating on the lava. The floating rubble was apparently so tough that it could withstand the extreme heat of the lava. Ben pressed an ice pack to his cheek. It was getting much hotter.

Sadie carefully slid down the inner sides of the volcano and then jumped down onto the biggest piece of floating stone, which swayed back and forth. She had slipped ice packs between the rope and her waist to withstand the heat, which was very strong now. It was a good idea, so Ben did the same. He used his "claws" to climb down to the same piece of rubble Sadie was on. He collapsed again on the piece of rubble, but then quickly jumped up. One of his ice packs fell off his waist and sunk into the bubbling lava with a sizzle. A magma bubble popped up, and embers sprayed around the volcano.

He wondered how Sadie was bearing the heat, even with the ice packs. He realized Jacob was down safely now. He finished coming down and followed Jacob over to where Sadie was.

"Look, the shards!" Sadie exclaimed. There were three sharp objects that looked like large pieces of glass that had been shattered. However, they looked like they were stained red. She picked up the three shards and handed one to each of the boys. There was also another scroll, which looked exactly like the first. Jacob picked it up. Ben was surprised the paper hadn't been scorched yet.

"I see something on that piece of rubble," Ben said. He leaped onto a piece of rubble, then another, with the shard held tightly in his hand. He slipped the sharp part between two of his fingers, so the shard wouldn't pierce his skin. His foot slipped on the rubble, and he fell, with his hand hovering inches away from the lava. The heat was almost unbearable now, but he tried to handle it. His hands were quaking as he picked up the sphere-shaped object, which was red with an orange fire shape at the bottom. It looked like an egg but was larger than any egg he had ever seen. Then Ben heard crackling, as the lava began to form a giant whirlpool, and Ben was afraid he might get sucked in.

CHAPTER III

Suddenly, the swirling stopped. But that wasn't even close to the end of Ben's troubles. As the lava rumbled, a huge red dragon emerged from the volcano. **"How dare you take my egg?!"** it growled in a deep, rasping voice. The rubble shook, and Jacob almost slipped into the lava.

"You can talk?" asked Ben, almost too in awe to speak. Then he cleared his throat and carefully said, "I'm sorry. I didn't realize. Please, take it back."

"Have it," the dragon roared. **"You are worthy. Take any other eggs you might happen to find. You deserve it."** And with that, the huge dragon sank back into the lava, with Ben not knowing at all what it meant, or how it even existed in the first place.

"What in the world of Epiconia was that?" Sadie gasped.

Ben carefully maneuvered himself on the rubble. "Guess what? I have a baby dragon now!" He stared down at the egg. "I think..."

"Not yet, it hasn't hatched yet," reasoned Jacob. "I'm going to read this next scroll."

Jacob unrolled it and read,

"To activate form, slap jewelry and say 'Pyromo.'
The first shard you found.
Next is Electricity.
To get it, have lightning strike
Your piece of jewelry."

Ben and Sadie touched their shards to their bracelet and brooch. Then Jacob did the same. The Fire Shard seemed to melt into the gem, which glowed a scarlet color before it turned all red.

Then Ben started climbing back up the volcano, followed by Jacob and Sadie. They slid back down the outside edge of the mountain and took off all their climbing equipment.

"Pyromo!" Ben said as he slapped his bracelet, following the scroll's instructions. Suddenly, he felt very hot, burning hot, maybe ninety degrees. His yellow shirt changed to red and became very ragged and torn. His sweatpants became tighter and turned red-orange. He also gained a cape that was the same color as his sweatpants. It had a picture of a small fire on it.

"Whoa!" Ben exclaimed. "I feel amazing!" With one hand tightly grasping the egg, he thrust out the other. A fireball, about the same size as a tennis ball, shot out of his palm and formed a hole in the volcano.

"What just happened?" they all asked at the same time.

Ben, still grasping his egg, looked up at the sky, which was cloudy and dark.

Jacob and Sadie said "Pyromo!" and changed forms like Ben had.

"I wouldn't do that if I were you," advised Ben. "It's starting to rain. The wetness will probably wash out our... powers, because we're in some... fire form."

"Well, we did it already," said Jacob. "On the other hand, we're lucky. If this is a thunderstorm, then we can get that second elemental power as soon as possible."

"But we don't know that this is a thunderstorm," reasoned Sadie.

BOOM!

Thunder rumbled above them.

"I think that answers your question, Sadie. We should probably get back home," Jacob started walking back.

Just then...

ZZZZZZRRAKK!

Lightning struck the top of the volcano. Rocks tumbled down. Small ones, then big ones, then HUGE ones!

"Run!" cried Ben. "Avalanche!"

CHAPTER IV

Ben ran and ran, not looking back to see the rocks tumbling after him, not even looking back to see if Jacob or Sadie made it out alive. He just kept running. He wasn't a very fast runner, but his panic made him go faster and faster.

A huge stone wall came into view. He halted, not thinking even about—who MADE this? If he tried to run around the wall, he figured the rocks would hit him before he could make it all the way around the wall. He turned back towards his siblings, because he couldn't keep on running. Jacob was close behind him, followed by Sadie.

He only had enough time left to worry.

"What are we going to do? We're going to DIE!" cried Ben, sobbing.

"I got it!" Sadie exclaimed happily. She put her claw-gloves back on and climbed over the wall. Jacob followed. Ben started climbing, but couldn't make it. He was just above the group of rocks when the biggest one provided just enough weight to topple the wall over.

SLAM!

The wall fell to the ground. However, they were on top of a hill. Portions of the wall, about the sizes of large sleds, zoomed down the hill as Ben held on with the claw-gloves.

They slid down the steep hill into a thick, dense forest that was lined with trees. The stone slab came to a stop, as did the rocks. Ben and his siblings carefully got down.

For the first time in a while, Ben looked down at his shirt. It was yellow again. He looked at Sadie's and Jacob's. Sadie's was back to pink while Jacob's was back to blue.

Then, Jacob cried, "Look! That's probably the tallest tree for miles!"

Jacob might have been right. The tree towered over their heads. It towered over all the other trees.

Ben realized he was soaking wet. He forgot that he was out in the rain—a thunderstorm, in fact. Ben ran under the tree, where he was covered by the leaves which shielded him from the pouring rain. The clouds weren't fluffy cotton candy anymore, they were dark boulders scattered across the sky. "Let's go!"

He set his egg at the base of the tree. Then he dug his claw-gloves into the hard tree trunk and hoisted himself up with one hand. He finally got up to the top of the tree, using his feet to propel himself further.

Jacob and Sadie followed him.

Ben carefully put his bracelet on a branch of the oak tree, and Jacob and Sadie did the same.

Then, again, something else that none of the siblings expected would happen, happened. All of the thunderclouds came together to form a huge body. A gigantic hand reached out and grabbed the three pieces of jewelry.

"Hey!" cried Jacob. "Give those back!"

"Why would I?" rumbled the cloud monster, forming a huge head with a cloud crown.

Is that Zeus? Ben thought.

"I am the Thunder God, a being of royalty. Why would you dare to leave these pieces of useless junk in my domain?"

"We're sorry," replied Jacob. "We wanted lightning to strike them. We're very sorry."

"Ha! You should be sorry!" the Thunder God bellowed. **"Lightning strikes are a sign of courtesy. It is a privilege for someone, or someTHING, to be struck by lightning. If I strike your jewels with lightning now, you will owe me a favor."**

"A favor?" Jacob asked. "Sure! What is it?"

"You will get me a perfectly rounded smooth yellow stone. If you don't by the end of this storm, then I will strike you, ALL OF YOU, with a bolt of lightning."

"Right!" Jacob slid back down the trunk, followed by Sadie and Ben last. They stepped a couple of feet away as the Thunder God put the jewelry back and got his hand ready.

ZZZZZRRAKK!

Lightning struck the tree, and it started to fall in Sadie, Ben, and Jacob's direction.

"Timber!" Jacob cried as he sprang to the side. Ben and Sadie jumped, too, in opposite directions.

CHAPTER V

The tree fell between Ben and Sadie. The lightning had also struck the pieces of jewelry at the top. The bracelet fell into Ben's hands, along with two yellow shards and a scroll.

Sadie caught her brooch and the amulet, which she handed to Jacob. She also caught another yellow shard, which she kept for herself. Ben tossed the second of his shards to Jacob.

Holding the shard and amulet, Jacob started running, yelling, "Come on! We have to find the yellow stone for the Thunder God!"

Sadie went in a different direction, and Ben went a third direction. They hoped by spreading out they would be able to look in more places.

Ben ended up at the beach. He saw how the rain made ripples on the ocean. Ben sighed and sat down to look at the beautiful ocean, forgetting about his task.

The peacefulness Ben felt was interrupted when he heard Jacob call out, "I found one!" Ben followed the sound of Jacob's voice until he met up with him. Sadie was also there; she must have turned around when she heard Jacob.

Jacob was crouched down, looking at the bottom of a tree. "There's a nice yellow stone here, along with something else. It looks like another egg."

Ben thought Jacob was probably right. This egg had the same shape as Ben's, but it was yellow and had a light blue lightning bolt shape at the bottom. Jacob stuffed the stone and the shard into his pocket and clutched the egg, being careful not to pierce the outer parts with his claw-gloves.

The trio sank their claw-gloves into a nearby tree and climbed the tree, but not to the top. Jacob hurled the stone into the air and cried out in desperation, "Here! Take the stone! Please, can you stop the thunderstorm?"

"Very well," bellowed the Thunder God. It picked up the yellow stone with its stormy hands. Then, the clouds that made up the Thunder God dissipated. With the Thunder God gone, the storm was gone, too

The three siblings weaved their way through the forest and ended up on the beach again.

"If this is the beach, then that forest must have been Beachy Forest," Sadie said.

That's an uncreative name, thought Ben.

"Isn't Beachy Forest the forest with the third biggest trees in the region?" asked Jacob to no one in particular.

"I'm going to read the scroll now," Ben said. He unrolled the scroll and read it out loud:

"To activate form, slap jewelry and say, 'Elecmo!'
After one comes two, and
After two comes three.

> **The third shard, the Water Shard,**
> **Is under the sea."**

Ben was ready to slap his bracelet when Jacob cried, "Hey! I'd like to do it first this time!"

Jacob touched the shard to his amulet and Ben and Sadie added the other shards to their gems shortly after. The gems, instead of turning all yellow like the three had expected, divided into two colors. Half of the gem stayed red and the other half turned yellow. Then Jacob slapped his amulet and said "Elecmo!"

Jacob's shirt turned yellow and slits in the sleeves formed. His dark blue denim jeans began to lighten and turn green until the color of his pants were turquoise. Jacob also got a turquoise cape with a yellow lightning bolt on it.

"This is so cool! Does this mean I can shoot lightning bolts out of my hands?"

He pumped one of his hands out (since the other was holding on to the dragon egg), like Ben did at Mt. Zekmo, and an electrical blast shot out of his hand. The blast disintegrated the low-hanging leaves of a nearby willow.

"Whoa!" He started running around excitedly. He realized he was running much faster than before. MUCH faster. He was so fast that in about two seconds, he was already about fifty yards away from his brother and sister. Ben barely could see him anymore, he was just a small yellow and blue blob in the distance. "Wow! I'm going so fast! I'm going at least fifty-five miles per hour, and the average adult human can only travel eight!"

"Apparently, you get super-fast intellect, too," Sadie quipped and rolled her eyes at her brother. However, she slapped her brooch and shouted, "Elecmo!"

"Elecmo!" Ben slapped his bracelet. It felt like a surge of electricity went through him, making him feel like his hair was standing on end. He stepped slowly. Fortunately, the super-speed only happened when they ran, so walking was fine.

Jacob kept running. He ran and skidded over the waves beyond the beach. "Hey! I can run on water!"

Ben realized Jacob's mistake before he did. When Jacob turned to talk, he stopped in the water for a short moment. That was all he needed to slowly start sinking under the water. He tried to run faster to get back on top, but the water just sucked him down.

Ben and Sadie waited for their brother to come up as they ran to the shore. They stood there for a couple seconds.

Jacob didn't come back up.

CHAPTER VI

"Jacob!" Ben cried.

Sadie was an expert swimmer. Ben and Jacob were both only mediocre. So, Sadie dived under the water.

Ben waded out to help, but when sea water splashed on his glasses, he could barely see anything. He thought he saw Sadie swimming toward where Jacob had gone under. Then he thought he saw Jacob sinking. Next to Jacob, he thought he saw a long, snake-like figure. But as Sadie pulled Jacob so he was firmly on shore, Ben wasn't sure if he had seen anything at all.

Jacob opened his eyes and looked down. His shirt was back to blue.

Ben's shirt was still yellow. But in the Electric Form his shirt was also yellow, so Ben looked at his drenched sweatpants. His pants were back to the way they had been. Ben's Electric Form time was already up, assuming they had a time limit in their forms.

Again, Ben felt a pull from the ocean that caused him to lose his train of thought. What was he doing? Something was important. Something like a mission.

Sadie came to the rescue again, this time mentally. "Guys, I think the next shard *is* under the water. It has to be. I thought the scroll was giving us a riddle or something—like the shard was at the bottom of a bottle of water—but it HAS to be under this ocean."

Ben shook himself and looked at Sadie. "Then how are we going to hold our breaths for that long?" he asked. "Jacob and I can't swim like you can."

"Let me put on my goggles and see," replied Sadie with a grin. She emphasized the word *goggles*. Because she loved to swim, she always had a pair of goggles in her pockets. Now it seemed less weird and more like a smart idea.

Sadie adjusted her goggles and dived back down under the water. After a few minutes, she popped her head up again. She was pretty far out in the ocean. "I couldn't see it. But it's probably farther out and very deep," she yelled.

She dived down again, but before long, she had swum back to shore. "I need to catch my breath," she said. "If only I had a snorkel or something."

Sadie went back out into the ocean. Jacob handed his egg to Ben so he could walk along the shoreline to find something that might help his sister. He didn't realize that Ben was staring off into the ocean again.

Ben set both eggs down beside him. He started off looking for the serpent and trying to keep an eye on Sadie in the water. But soon, the water made him forget about the mission and his responsibility.

Jacob used his power to speed down the shoreline. He was able to find an oxygen tank and snorkel on a lifeguard's chair. What luck! But though the snorkel was light, the tank was heavy, and he couldn't use his power while carrying it. He made his way back to Ben and Sadie.

Something brushed past Sadie in the water. Sadie turned to the shore to see a large serpent speeding toward Ben and the dragon eggs.

She started to shout, "Watch out!" but a wave hit her in the face and knocked her down under the water. She quickly swam back up to the surface and came up spluttering. Sadie saw the serpent knock Ben over and grab the eggs.

"Oh, no! The eggs!" she cried.

CHAPTER VII

Ben sat up. "What?" He looked around. The eggs were gone. The thing that had knocked him down was swimming away. "Oh, no! The eggs! Oh, no! Sadie!"

The serpent swam around Sadie while Ben looked on in horror. It rose to the surface and flicked water with its tail. Then, before Sadie even had time to say anything, it wrapped its tail around her and yanked her out of the water.

"I am the King of the Sssssserpentssssss. What do you want? Why have you come here? Have you come for," the serpent paused, "the treasssssure? Everybody wantsssss the treasssssure." The serpent tightened its grip.

"Treasure? You took our—" she paused in thought, "--*their* eggs. We want them back!" Sadie said.

"Eggsssss? They are my eggsssss, not your eggsssss. I found them on the ssssshore. Eggsssss on the ssssshore are mine. They are my eggsssss." The Serpent King tightened its grip on Sadie.

Sadie managed to sputter, "We're sorry, Serpent King. You need dragon eggs to stay immortal, don't you? You can keep them." Sadie realized that she needed to be willing to sacrifice the eggs to keep the food chain—and world—in balance.

The Serpent King relaxed its grip on Sadie. They were still face to face, and Sadie could breathe again, but didn't feel like she was going to be dropped into the water with a loud *SPLOOSH*, either.

"You have proved yoursssssself. Take the eggsssss. I will find more." The Serpent King gently set Sadie back into the water. The eggs appeared in a bubble, and then the Serpent King's tail gently guided the bubble to the shore. Jacob and Ben waded into the water to collect their eggs. The bubble popped as soon as they touched it. Then, the Serpent King was gone.

Where the Serpent King had been, Sadie looked in the water and saw a chest. It had to be the "treasssssure" the king of snakes was talking about. She dived under the water and reached for the chest. It wasn't too heavy, so she dragged it behind her to the shore to Ben and Jacob, who were gaping in awe.

The chest opened easily, and Sadie carefully handed Ben and Jacob each a blue shard from inside. She found a third dragon egg, which her brothers agreed she should keep for herself. There was also another scroll. This scroll glowed purple, and seemed completely dry; it must have been enchanted to not get wet. She sat down on the beach, unrolled the scroll, and read:

"To activate form, slap jewelry and say 'Aquamo!'

To master the power on your neck,
Your chest or your wrist,
You need to find the Plant Shard
Hidden in Beachy Forest."

"Why are there shards around the same place?" Jacob asked.

"Well, we could have gone anywhere high to get our pieces of jewelry struck by lightning. Then, we could have traveled to an ocean on the other side of the world..." Sadie might have continued ranting, but her brother stopped her.

"We get the idea," Ben said. "Anyway, we have some time to spare, so why don't we take a break from our 'adventure' and practice our powers?"

"Let's do this!" Jacob said.

CHAPTER VIII

"I'll test Pyromo first," Ben said.

He was standing in front of a large boulder. The three managed to work out that they wanted only one power to break the boulder for each person, especially since everyone wanted to be good at a different power, though they could all use all the powers.

"Pyromo," Ben said, slapping his bracelet. His clothes changed, like they did last time. He shot a fiery blast out of his hand. The blast surrounded the boulder and slowly broke it.

"Nice!" Ben said. "Pyromo bro—obliterated it." He had wanted to use the word *obliterated* for a long time, but he had never found the chance. "Jacob, you're up."

Jacob turned to another large boulder nearby. Because Ben broke the first boulder with Pyromo, he slapped his amulet and said, "Elecmo!"

A lightning bolt shot out of his hands and hit the boulder, causing it to shatter like a piece of glass.

All three touched their most recently obtained shards to the gem, and once again, the shards melted into the gem.

Sadie was the first to change into the Water Form. "Aquamo!" she cried as she slapped her brooch. Her blouse turned blue and her skirt turned purple. Her leggings turned blue, too. She gained a cape that was purple with a picture of a blue water drop on it. Her hands developed bubbles around them as well. She placed her egg in the sand and shot her hand out. A huge bubble shot out of her hand, and it surrounded another large boulder without popping, despite it being a bubble.

"That's it?" Jacob shouted. "Aquamo is weak!"

The bubble floated upwards with the boulder inside... but only for about two seconds. Then...

POP!

The bubble seemed to explode, and the boulder fell. But the boulder didn't break in two. Instead a large crack formed through its middle. Sadie mumbled something that Ben couldn't quite make out. Then she waved her other hand and shot a jet of water out of her palm. The boulder broke in half. She murmured something inaudible again. Eventually, she changed back to her normal form.

"That was... um, cool," said Jacob. "But I still like Elecmo better. Elecmo!" he said as he slapped his amulet. Then he zoomed off into the distance, clutching his egg and saying, "Come on! Follow me! I want to do something!"

"Should we follow?" asked Sadie.

"Why not?" answered Ben. "Elecmo!"

He grabbed his egg and zoomed off into the distance. Ben could just make out Jacob, a yellow blob in the distance, so he followed him. Jacob zoomed left and right, back and forth. Ben was dodging trees, jumping over rocks and swinging on vines for what seemed like hours.

Suddenly, Jacob stopped. Ben realized he wasn't wearing yellow anymore, and guessed that Jacob's clothes had turned back to blue when he had used up his electric power.

He stopped just behind Jacob. "Hey, where were you going?"

"I was trying to go back to the cave in our backyard," Jacob panted, "but we're not even halfway there. We're in the middle of a forest!" He turned around. "Hi, Sadie!"

Sadie collapsed on the ground as her Elecmo power wore off. She rolled onto her back and looked up. "It's getting dark. We should stay here for the night."

"What would Mom and Dad say?"

"They won't care," Sadie replied, and Ben thought she was wrong.

Ben zoomed away. He plucked lots of leaves off a tree and used tree sap to bind them together. Then he ripped them into three pieces and threw them to the side. He grabbed a vine and pulled. It didn't budge. He pulled harder. Still nothing. He looked behind him and saw a pair of gleaming red eyes.

CHAPTER IX

Ben slowly stepped back. The creature looked passive and calm. As his eyes adjusted to the night, he could see the animal was a feline with pitch-black stripes and a long tail. A long, green tail.

That's what I must have been pulling, Ben thought.

It couldn't be a tiger, even though it sure looked like one, because it wasn't orange. It was green with black stripes.

Ben stepped forward. The big cat blinked at him. He stroked the animal's ears. Then he beckoned it to follow him. He started running.

He wasn't going really fast, so he must have gone back to normal.

He ducked below a low-hanging branch. He wondered if the cat was following him, but he didn't dare look. It was cold and he shivered. Had he really run so far into the forest when he was in Electric Form?

He kept running until he saw Jacob and Sadie. They were zooming around, swiftly weaving vines and leaves into comfortable beds. Jacob spread out a blanket made of leaves and lay down. Sadie was still weaving her blanket when she saw Ben and the creature.

She jumped, but she didn't look scared, and kept on weaving. "What do you have there?" she asked.

"I don't know," replied Ben. "What is it?" he said jokingly, but realistically too.

Sadie pulled a tiny book from the pocket in her blouse. *She sure carries a lot of strange stuff everywhere,* Ben thought. He read the title on the front of the book. *A Book of Rare and Mythological Creatures.* "I can't read this without light," she complained.

"I can fix that," Ben said. "Pyromo!" He tossed a tiny fireball out of his hands and created a small fire. "Does that help?" he said somewhat sarcastically.

Sadie flipped through the pages lighted by the fire until she found the one she wanted. She read, "The Natiger—pronounced Nuh-TY-gur—is a—"

"That's not a very creative name," interrupted Ben.

"Can you let me finish?" said Sadie. She kept reading, "—is a very rare creature descended from tigers. It or—"

"So THAT'S why it has the stripes!" Ben interrupted again.

"PLEASE just let me finish!" Sadie exclaimed.

"Okay, okay!"

"—originated when the tigers' fur was not enough to protect them from the cold, so they rolled around in leaves, grass, and vines to keep themselves warmer. When the nature-coated tiger mated with others, the grass, leaves and vines merged with their descendants. Their fur turned green and the vines became very helpful in grabbing other objects, so useful that Natigers nowadays rarely ever use their legs to do anything other than walking. The Nat—"

Ben interrupted Sadie once more. "This must be a Natiger!" he cried.

Ben stroked the Natiger's back, but the Natiger turned away from him and ran into the forest.

"Wait! Come back!" cried Ben. He ran after the Natiger.

Sadie sighed, put the book back in her blouse, and ran to catch up.

Ben kept on running and running. The Natiger was a green blob in the distance in front of him. This chase distinctly reminded Ben of the previous chase in the late afternoon of the same day. But then...

PLOP!

Ben's right leg sunk into some black gooey substance. The tree next to him was coated in it, too. He stared at the tree.

Then he noticed that the huge tree next to him was sinking into the black gooey substance that he was stuck in.

Ben gasped. Was he going to sink, too?

CHAPTER X

Ben tried to yank his leg out of the sticky black goo, but it was no use. His legs were fully surrounded by it, and it was making its way up his chest.

I'm not going to make it out alive, Ben thought. *Just like my dream. It is the same thing, isn't it?*

Then he heard soft footsteps drumming behind him. He turned his head.

"Sadie!" he cried. "Thank goodness! I'm sinking!"

"What is that stuff?" she asked.

Ben just stared at her, helplessly, making puppy-dog eyes.

"Never mind that," she replied in response to herself. She grabbed Ben's hand.

She pulled really hard and Ben flew out of the black goo. Unfortunately, Ben landed headfirst against a big rock.

"Ow!" he cried.

Sadie flopped down next to the goo, panting. "Why am I the one that has to save everyone?"

Ben squeezed the goo out of his shirt onto the grass and wiped some of it off of his sweatpants. He got up and started running (in circles, because he hit his head, and is covered in goo), trying to find the Natiger. Then all of a sudden...

ZAP!

Ben got shocked, like a static shock in the winter.

"Just where do you think you're going?" Sadie asked. Electricity surged from her index finger. Ben noticed she was in her Electric Form.

"I was TRYING to find the Natiger," Ben said.

"What for?"

"I wanted to see...um...okay. I don't know." Ben sighed. "I was just interested."

"Well, you're not going anywhere without me," Sadie replied. "You seriously need me. Am I the only mature one around here?"

You are *the oldest, so yes*, Ben thought. But he wouldn't dare say that out loud. "No," he insisted. Then he ran off, looking for the Natiger.

"Wait for me!" Sadie zoomed in her Electric Form.

Ben was almost literally blown away by Sadie's speed. He had forgotten about her use of the Electric Form.

"No! You wait for me!" he called to her. He slapped his bracelet and cried, "Elecmo!"

He ran for a couple seconds, then realized he should probably tell Jacob where he and Sadie were. He zoomed back to the temporary camp to fill Jacob in. It took him less than a minute. When he got to the camp, he saw Jacob frantically scrambling around, looking for something.

"Jacob!"

Jacob jumped, and then sighed. "Ben! I was looking all over for you!" He sighed again. "But wait. Where's Sadie?"

"We're looking for the Natiger."

"Cool! Elecmo!" Jacob slapped his amulet so he could speed off with Ben, even though he probably had no idea what a Natiger was.

Jacob and Ben caught up to Sadie, who had stopped at the river to consider it cautiously. She carefully stepped across a rock and bounded over another two.

"We can run on water, Sadie," Jacob dashed to the other side in two split seconds. "See?" He shouted across the river at Sadie.

Ben followed quickly after Jacob. "I did it too, Sadie. There's nothing to worry about."

"Better safe than sorry," Sadie replied. She stepped carefully on to another stone. She was a good swimmer, but the river current was very strong. She wasn't taking any chances. She carefully made her way across the river and joined Ben and Jacob.

No sooner had both of Sadie's feet hit the opposite beach, Ben touched his pointer finger to her arm.

ZAP!

She plopped onto the dirt. "Mmphlgh!" Sadie straightened herself and wiped mud off her face. "What was that for?"

"Payback," Ben grinned.

CHAPTER XI

The trio strolled through the large forest, figuring that they were close to the Natiger's den. Ben parted two clumps of bushes. "Look," he whispered. "The Natiger!"

The Natiger was looking for something. It pushed a fragile tree back and scooped up a small gold coin. The Natiger dropped the coin into a small pile.

The pile was made up of many small shiny trinkets, including coins, ribbons, and...

"Look! The Shards!" Ben cried.

Ben could barely make out the color among the other shiny stuff and the darkness of the night. But if he had to guess, he would have said they were dark green. The trio of shards were at the top of the pile, with a scroll tied together by a shiny (Ben guessed it was red since the others were as well) ribbon.

Ben sneaked up and then hid behind a tree when the Natiger glanced at him. He ducked under a bush and reached his arm toward the pile.

Almost there, he thought.

Just then, the Natiger turned and pounced on Ben.

Ben struggled under the Natiger's weight. He spit a tuft of green hair out of his mouth. He tugged on the Natiger's fur, trying to get out from under it, but it was no use.

"Guys?" He called. "A little help here?"

"If you had let me finish reading, I would have said that the Natiger only gets aggressive when defending its territory," Sadie sighed.

Jacob hesitated at first, but then he came running. He grabbed the vine attached to the Natiger's left shoulder and tugged.

He noticed that it looked like Sadie was thinking. She sat down.

Ben sighed. He thrust the creature off him and grabbed the shards. "Run!" he cried.

Jacob and Ben started running. "Come on!" Jacob said.

Sadie still sat there, though.

The Natiger used its vines and grabbed Jacob and Sadie.

"Why didn't it grab you?" Jacob asked Ben.

"Who knows? Pyromo!" Ben slapped his bracelet.

Ben shot tiny sparks of fire out of his left hand, which the Natiger brushed off with its tail.

"Just HELP US!" Jacob cried.

"What else can I do?" Ben asked.

"Something with offensive capabilities!" Jacob suggested.

"Fine!" Ben answered. He shot a huge jet of fire out of both hands. It burned the Natiger's fur, turning it from green to a dark, ashy gray. The Natiger loosened the vines and whimpered.

Jacob and Sadie toppled out of the Natiger's grip.

Neither of them were very thankful. "I could have saved myself," Sadie said. She brushed some ash off her skirt.

"You almost KILLED me!" Jacob complained. "Plus, you ruined our clothes."

Just then, Ben noticed that Jacob's clothes (and Sadie's) were now stained gray, and their hair was bent back.

"You're welcome," Ben replied sarcastically. "Do you know what I think?" He didn't wait for a response. "I think we should bring this Natiger on our adventures."

Sadie gasped. Jacob pretended to faint.

"Are you crazy?" Jacob cried as he sat back up again.

"Why not?"

"It's hostile, it's angry specifically at us, and our gems are shiny, so it will probably attack us." He counted on his fingers.

"Yes, but it COULD really help us."

"No," Sadie and Jacob said in unison. "Absolutely not."

"But--"

"No, final answer," Sadie snapped. And then she left. Ben and Jacob slowly followed.

CHAPTER XII

The trio was walking for a while, since Jacob insisted they should go back to the cave from earlier and get the crystals that were there.

Once, Ben heard a rustling in the leaves. He turned around and saw a shape that he recognized, but it darted away before Ben could tell what it was. He was able to make out three vine-like shapes.

"Uh, guys? I think the Na--" Ben started.

"I guess I was wrong when I said, 'We're not even halfway there'," Jacob interrupted. Finally, they came across a cave, which Ben recognized but couldn't point out. Ben and Sadie prepared to walk around to the mouth of the cave. But Jacob climbed over the back, jumped down at the mouth of the cave and ran inside. "It's more fun this way!" he called.

"You know what? We never even opened this scroll," said Ben, as he took off the red ribbon and unraveled the scroll. He read,

"To activate form, slap jewelry and say 'Plantamo.'
If you wish to master the elements,
The fifth shard you must crave.
The Earth Shard is hidden in the forbidden Demon's Cave."

"Demon's Cave?!" Sadie exclaimed. "That's FORBIDDEN!"

"I can tell," Ben replied, "it says so here," and he tossed it to Sadie. "I want to try this out!" he cried. He ran into the cave, following Jacob. Then Ben slapped his bracelet and cried "Plantamo!" The gem had split into four equal parts, one of them dark green, showing that he could now transform into a Plant Form.

Ben's shirt and shoes turned lime green, and his sweatpants turned dark green, along with the cape he grew, which had a lime green picture of a leaf on it.

"I wonder what I can do in THIS form," said Ben as he flicked his wrist. A large vine, much like the one on the Natiger's shoulder, grew from Ben's palm and grabbed the largest crystal on the wall.

"Why don't we grab it?" suggested Jacob. "After all, we finished exploring the cave." For a moment, Ben wondered, *What cave?* But then he realized this was the cave in his backyard.

Sadie stepped back, and Jacob and Ben pulled as hard as they could, but the crystal didn't break. Instead, it moved lower on the wall like a light switch, and a trapdoor opened, swallowing Ben and Jacob.

"It was a secret lever!" Jacob cried.

"Oooooof course," Ben said sarcastically, rolling his eyes.

Sadie turned into her Water Form, as the trio called it, and waved her hand. A huge bubble surrounded Ben and Jacob, like the time she had encased the boulder with another bubble, and slowly lifted them up. The trapdoor swiftly shut below them.

"It was a trap!" Jacob panted once the bubble popped.

"Thanks," Ben added.

Sadie sighed. "It's hard being the smart one."

"Anyway, let's get the other crystals!" Ben cried. He used the same vine to grab another crystal on the right side of the wall and pulled. Then he realized the mistake he just made and sighed.

The same thing happened, but instead of a trapdoor, lava dropped down from the ceiling. Sadie shot a jet of water out of her palm and quickly extinguished the flames. "Don't you see?" she exclaimed. "This cave is all a trap! Someone built a cave, and set traps all over the place to—to try and kill us!"

"But why did they pick us?" Ben asked. "And why are there, like, prizes at the end?"

"That I never thought about," replied Sadie. "But what I DO know—is that there's someone on our tail, and someone not on our side."

CHAPTER XIII

The trio had agreed to stock up on supplies, including their backpacks, water, and a heater for their eggs, at home first, which they did (again, without their parents noticing). Then they headed towards Demon's Cave.

Ben looked up through the trees. Judging by the sun's position in the sky, it was noon, because the sun was the highest in the sky. At one point, he turned around to see how far they had come, and was sure he had seen a suspicious figure darting through the undergrowth.

"Guys, you know when you said not to bring the Natiger along? I think he's coming anyway. . ." said Ben nervously.

"We're here!" Sadie seemed to ignore him.

"Already?" Ben asked.

Sadie shrugged and wandered into the cave, ducking under the CAUTION tape surrounding the mouth of the cave. "Savor the light," she advised. "It's the last you'll see for a long, long time."

"What's that supposed to mean?" Jacob asked, noticing more of the black gooey substance to his right.

"Um... because we're going into a dark cave..." she awkwardly laughed.

"But you said—oh, forget it." Jacob kept on walking. "Ben, you coming?"

"It's ARE you coming," Ben corrected him, "and... I just feel weird about going in a cave that... well, the last person who came in here never made it out alive!" Ben remembered reading from a book about famous places.

"None of those people had elemental powers. Come on!"

Ben thought Jacob sounded too confident for this cave. But Ben kept walking, and soon, they were halfway in.

Soon enough, they found a little pool surrounded by stalagmites. On the other side of the pool was a little ledge, with three small orange shards and two scrolls resting on it.

"Okay, I admit, that was easier than I thought," said Ben, as he reached out to see if he could grab the shard without crossing the pool.

"Aquamo!" Sadie cried as she slapped her brooch.

"I suppose that will help you swim faster?" Ben cocked his head to one side, unsure of why Sadie turned into her Water Form. But Sadie shot a jet of water out of her palm and hit the top of the cave. "What are you doing?" Ben asked.

A huge boulder fell from the top of the cave and landed just in front of Sadie. Ben and Jacob jumped in the pool to avoid it.

Then Sadie moved her hand and grabbed an imaginary object. The pool transformed into a hand and tugged onto Ben's bracelet. It broke, and the hand tossed it over the boulder into Sadie's hand. She did the same thing with Jacob's necklace. "Hey!" he cried.

Sadie looked satisfied. Then she took the two gems out of their spots and laid them on the floor before walking away.

CHAPTER XIV

"Sadie!" Ben screamed. "Why did you DO that...?"

"Ben!" Jacob cried. "The water is rising. When the boulder fell, it must have created a crack in the ground that led to a lake! The cave is flooding! If the water reaches up above our heads, we'll *drown*!"

"Grab on!" Ben cried. He heaved himself up to the ledge where the shards lay. Jacob followed, but the ledge looked like it was just about to collapse.

"Look!" said Jacob. "The water is pushing the boulder!" Jacob was right. The force of the water was nudging the boulder to the side. Jacob grabbed the shards and scrolls, dived in the water, and shoved the boulder. That extra nudge sent it toppling out of the cave. The water gushed out of the tunnel after the boulder. Jacob climbed out of the pool.

"My amulet!" he cried.

In one swift jump, Ben landed next to Jacob and picked up his bracelet. "I'm surprised she didn't take them," Ben said. But then he saw the gems. They were split into two. In a huge amount of shock, he took the scrolls from Jacob (which were tied with an unusual green ribbon) and read the first one. He read,

"To activate form, slap jewelry and say Terramo."

"That was short," he said. He read the next one, which said,

"Magical gems can be repaired with the sap from the Tree of Life.

**There were five who controlled
the elements
Who had the power of the stars
But one of them will become a
great threat
And One, Two, Three, and Four
must stop it from afar.
Then will the world be at peace
once more.
And great power will be fully
restored."**

"Sounds like a prophecy," said Jacob. "Here's what I got from it—you and I are One and Two, and Sadie is Five—the great threat. We need to find Three and Four—whoever they are—and stop our sister."

You're quick to suspect her, Ben thought. But out loud he only said, "Hm." Then he looked at Jacob. "Well, what are we waiting for? Let's go!"

Soon enough, they were outside, having picked up the shards, jewelry and gem fragments.

"Wherc's the Natiger?" asked Jacob.

More importantly, where's Sadie? Ben thought. He wasn't ready to accept that his sister was the evil one. *Even more importantly, who are the third and fourth people? Where are they? We don't even know where to look!* But he didn't speak his thoughts out loud. He just said, "Well, for now, let's just go to the Tree of Life and get some sap to repair our gems."

The two transformed into their Electric Forms and zoomed off.

CHAPTER XV

The Tree of Life was not as far away as they thought. In about fifteen minutes, they could see it. However, the Tree of Life was incredibly large, and it towered above all the other trees, with its topmost leaves almost touching the clouds.

"Looks like a willow," Jacob said. "See how those branches are so low? We could probably jump up and grab them."

As they got closer, they could see a little shape climbing the tree. Ben assumed it was probably an animal or person.

As they got even closer, they realized it was a person. A girl, in fact, with blond hair streaked with blue, in pigtails, wearing a red dress.

The trio—no, now duo—found themselves in an oak forest, which they quickly navigated their way through. And then, they were face-to-face with the Tree of Life.

"Well, let's start climbing," said Ben.

He grabbed some of the trunk that stuck out and pulled himself up. *One foot down, five-thousand more to go,* he thought.

For the first one-hundred feet, the trunk was slanted at about a forty-degree angle. Jacob and Ben climbed up that relatively quickly.

Then for another fifty feet, it was slanted at a forty-five-degree angle. Ben eyed the girl. She was now knocking sap out of the tree. Ben and Jacob caught up with the girl. She poured the sap into a bottle and shut the lid.

Ben was cautious to speak to her, because he didn't know at all what she was like. Jacob spoke for him, though. "What are you doing?" Jacob asked.

"Getting sap from this tree," she replied.

Obviously, Ben thought.

"My name's Josie," she added, "what's yours?"

"Jacob," Jacob said.

"Ben," Ben said.

"What are you here for?" Josie asked. "I'm getting some sap to use for when I get hurt."

"What do you mean, 'when I get hurt'?" Ben asked.

"Didn't you know sap from the Tree of Life heals?" she replied. She uncovered two more bottles full of sap behind her. "Want some?"

Jacob took a bottle. "Thanks," he said.

Josie handed a bottle to Ben, too. "Don't worry," she said, "I have plenty!"

Ben shook the bottle. "What do you do?"

"Drink it!" she replied, like everybody in the world knew, but not at all meanly.

Ben felt a little baffled by this idea, but before he could ask any questions, she changed the subject.

"What are those big lumps in your backpacks?" she asked. "They're glowing!"

"They are?" Ben took his backpack off. *The eggs! They ARE glowing! Are they hatching?* Ben thought, and took his egg out. Jacob took his backpack off too, and took his egg out. It was also glowing.

"They're eggs," said Jacob, "and it looks like they're about to hatch."

CHAPTER XVI

"What a good place for them to hatch!" exclaimed Josie enthusiastically as she clapped her hands. "The Tree of Life's sap can make them healthy and strong as soon as they break out of their eggs!"

CRACK!

Ben's egg hatched first. A small red baby dragon emerged. The dragon was curled up, and its head was about as big as an apple. It had tiny wings, too, and a tail with a small flame marking on it. It even had curved brown horns.

Jacob's newly-hatched dragon looked fairly similar, but it was yellow, and it had a lightning bolt mark on its tail.

"I wonder if the dragons can fly?" asked Jacob.

"Ja-cob!" Ben put emphasis on his name. "They're just babies! They can't fly yet!"

Jacob unscrewed the bottle that Josie had given him. He stuck his finger in the sap and let his dragon lick it off. "Ew!" Ben said.

"So cute!" Josie exclaimed. "What are you going to name them?"

Ben stared at his dragon. It was red, with dark brown horns and tail. It was a fire dragon, Ben noticed, matching the shard it was found with, and it was quite hot. "How about... Magma?" Ben stroked his dragon, then instantly regretted it because he almost got burned. He tried to shake off the pain.

"That's a great name!" exclaimed Josie. "What about you, Jacob? What is your dragon's name?"

"Bolt," replied Jacob. He clearly had been thinking about this for quite a long time.

"Cool!" said Josie. Then she looked at Jacob's amulet. "Cool necklace!" she exclaimed. "Where did you get it?"

"Well, I found it in a cave," Jacob answered. "Ben got his bracelet there too," he added.

"Hey! I got these earrings in a cave too!" Josie touched her earrings. This was the first time Ben noticed Josie's large earrings that dangled down to her shoulders. They were stone-gray, like Ben's bracelet and Jacob's amulet, and they each also had a gem inside them. However, the gems were all white.

"How?" Ben asked, suspiciously.

"Well, when I had breakfast two days ago," she started off, "this number came though my window." She imitated a fluttering piece of paper, "Six-one-three, I think. And when I went outside, there was this cave, with a really, really, long hall. So, then there was this tic-tac-toe board of buttons. I pressed six-one-three on it, like the note said. It opened, and there was this pair of earrings and a scroll. So—"

Ben interrupted her. "That's exactly what happened to us!"

"Hey, cool!" Josie pumped her first in the air. "Look! I got this power and I can fly!" She touched her left earring and said, "Breezemo!" Josie pronounced it "bree-ZEM-oh."

The top part of Josie's red dress turned white, along with her shoes, and the bottom half of her dress turned light gray, along with a cape of the same color that had a cloud on it. She soared into the air, and her long hair brushed the willow-like leaves of the tree.

"See?!" she shouted down to Ben, Jacob and the dragons.

"I can use powers too!" yelled Ben, as he slapped his bracelet. Then he remembered the problem. "Oh yeah. My gem is broken."

"I can help!" Josie playfully exclaimed. She drifted down to Ben and pulled a bottle of glue out of her backpack. She uncapped the glue and poured some Life Sap into the bottle. Ben handed her the two halves of his gem, and Josie then glued them together, doing the same with Jacob's right after.

81

"That was SO much easier than I thought," said Jacob.

"I figured that normal glue wouldn't work, so I combined Life Sap and the glue," Josie said proudly. "It worked. Life Sap can pretty much do anything."

"Thanks," Ben said.

He transformed into his Fire Form and playfully shot a jet of fire out of his hand. The flame nearly missed Josie's cape.

"Hey!" she playfully cried, and dived toward Ben. Ben dodged and slid down the tree trunk. On the ground, Ben noticed that the dragons were "playing" too. Magma sent a breath of fire towards Bolt, and Bolt zoomed away from the flames. Ben took a moment to make sure there were warm and dry places for the dragons to settle down as well as a variety of greens to eat when they finished playing.

Jacob slid down the tree and took a shard out of his pocket. *I never put this in the gem,* he thought, and slipped the orange shard into the gem.

The gem split into the five first colors of the rainbow—red, orange, yellow, green and blue.

He slapped his amulet and cried, "Terramo!"

CHAPTER XVII

Jacob's shirt and shoes turned orange, his jeans turned a color Jacob thought was maroon, and he gained a cape of the same color with an orange equilateral triangle on it. Jacob assumed it was supposed to represent a mountain. He placed Bolt down on the base of the colossal tree and joined the playful fight.

Josie waved her hand and a gust of wind blew Ben backward. He fought back by shooting another jet of fire out of his hand which grazed Josie's dyed-blue hair.

Jacob raised his hand to test out his new power. The chunk of earth below Ben's feet rose and he was lifted into the air, although not as high as Josie was in the sky, which was almost as high as the lowest clouds.

Jacob shook his hand, and the chunk below Ben's feet vibrated back and forth.

"Co-o-o-o-m-e o-o-o-n-n J-a-a-a-c-o-o-o-b," Ben cried as his voice vibrated, "s-t-t-o-o-o-p-p t-h-a-a-a-t-t!"

Jacob lowered his hand and the rock lowered to its rightful place in the ground with a CHUNK! He flicked his wrist, and a small rock was launched from his knuckles and hit Ben square in the forehead.

"Ow!" Ben rubbed his head where the rock hit him. "Hey!"

"Sorry," Jacob said in an atypically somewhat sarcastic tone. Then he pulled his fist back, as if he could undo the motion he just made.

Then something unexpected happened. All the rocks on the surface within five yards in front of Jacob tore out of the ground and attached to Jacob's hand, forming a giant fist.

Ben stepped back as the rocks beneath his feet rose out of the ground and added to Jacob's giant hand.

"Whoa!" Jacob cried. "Now THIS is cool!" He slowly lifted his hand up. It wasn't as heavy as he thought it would be, despite all the rocks attached to it. Then he slammed it back down again. He forgot to lower it slowly.

Sheets of dust clouded Jacob's vision, and the earth rippled below him. However, there wasn't much earth to ripple, as most of the earth within five yards in front of Jacob had been ripped from the ground and was on his fist. Then the huge fist disappeared.

Jacob looked back at his clothes. He was back to his normal form. He looked to the ground, which was a flat plane. "Wait," he exclaimed, "if I'm not in my form anymore, how is Josie still in hers?"

"I'm not," Josie said.

Jacob noticed that she was lying in a pile of damp and squishy moss, and assumed that her Sky Form time had run out.

The moss was next to a puddle of the weird black goo. Josie reached toward it. "What is this stuff?" she said.

"No!" Ben exclaimed, "that's—"

Josie stuck her finger in it. The goo clung to her immediately.

"—really sticky," Ben mumbled. He pulled Josie's finger out with a few quick tugs.

Josie's finger still had some of the black goo on it. "What'd it feel like"? Jacob asked. He had never touched the goo before, and never dared to try.

"Kind of like some kind of force was pulling me down," she replied.

Jacob remembered how Ben had told him about the tree being swallowed by the goo.

Then she added, "It felt like it was pulling me, kind of like a current."

"I wonder where the current goes," Jacob said to no one in particular. He took a tennis ball out of his backpack and dropped it into the pool of goo. It instantly headed to the left. Then Jacob noticed it extended like a river, twisting and turning. It stopped at the base of the Tree of Life. Then Jacob looked up.

The Tree of Life! It was fully infected by the goo! It was covered in the weird black ooze. Bolt and Magma jumped off as it shriveled. It hung down, its huge leaves brushing the ground, even lower than before. Then it fully disintegrated and turned into a large pile of dust, unlike Jacob had expected.

The wind blew it away.

CHAPTER XVIII

"Whoa. . .," Ben stammered.

Josie looked down at her canteen. "I guess this is the last sap from the Tree of Life." She paused. "Maybe... ever."

Ben looked down at his own canteen. "Yeah." He shook it, even though he already knew it was almost full. "We're going to have to use this wisely."

"I have something to give you," Josie said. "I know this isn't the best time, but..." She reached into her pocket and pulled out four white shards. "When I found these, there were five shards. I didn't know who to give them to, because no one I knew could use them. But you can use them, right?" Josie cocked her head to one side.

"Sure!" Jacob said, and then took a shard. "Wow, thanks!" He took another one and handed it to Ben. "But who does this last one go to?" Jacob added. There was still another shard in Josie's hand.

Josie looked down at it. "I... don't know," she replied.

Ben thought for a second. *Could it... no. That's... impossible!*

Josie interrupted Ben's thought by continuing. "But... where are we going? What are we going to do now?"

"That's obvious," Ben said, like he knew everything. "We save the Tree of Life!"

"But—how?" Jacob pointed out. "We don't have a clue about what to do anyway!" Then he heard a SCREEEECH! He swiveled around and saw Magma and Bolt stuck in the black goo. He quickly ran to yank them out.

"Okay, this stuff is REALLY getting on my nerves," Jacob murmured. He scooped a sample of it into a beaker, "What is this black stuff?"

"Where did you get that beaker?" asked Ben.

Jacob ignored Ben's question. "I just wish I knew what it was. Some kind of... slime?"

Then it popped into Ben's mind. "According to Sadie's book of rare and mythological creatures, the black goo is Shadowstalker Ooze, invented by—" he thought of the name and shuddered, "—Shadowstalker... for—actually, I don't know why."

"I have lots of questions," Jacob said. "I thought that was just a myth! And most importantly," he added a long pause, "why were--why are--you reading Sadie's book?!"

CHAPTER XIX

"Umm...," Ben mumbled, scratching his arm.

"What?" Jacob asked. "Do you miss her? She BETRAYED us, remember?"

Ben wanted to answer *Yes* and *I know*, but he didn't.

"Who's Sadie?" Josie asked.

"She is... our sister." Ben was suddenly very interested in his toes. "She was the one who smashed our gems—I think."

"Oh..." said Josie. "Well, think of it this way. If Sadie had never crushed your gems, then you never would have met me, and you never would have healed your gems!"

"If Sadie had never cracked our gems, then they would never have needed to be healed," Jacob pointed out.

"Well, that's true," Josie replied. "But—"

Ben stood between the two. "Come on guys, stop stalling! We have to solve this mystery!"

"Uh, guys? What about your drag--" asked Josie.

"YOU still never answered the question I asked you," Jacob snapped at Ben.

"Does it MATTER?" Ben groaned, in an exasperated manner. "Let's just focus on the task at hand."

"That WAS the task at hand!"

Josie transformed into her Sky Form. "Come on!" she said. "While you two were bickering, I scooped up the dragons and put them in a safe place. Then I tracked the location of the producer of Shadowstalker Ooze on my phone. Follow me!" She zoomed off through the trees.

"Should we follow her?" Jacob asked.

"Why not?" Ben replied, and slipped the white shard into the gem. It split into five—red, yellow, green, blue and white. Then he took an orange shard out of his pocket and added it to the five, creating six.

"Let's go!" he cried. "Breezemo!" He jumped up, but never came back down. He looked at the ground. He was flying! He twirled around in the air. Then he realized: how DID he fly? Right now, he was just levitating. He started trying to walk, but he didn't move. It just felt like treading water.

Wait, that's it, Ben thought. *Treading water! Flying is just like swimming.*

He swept his arm over his head, then kicked, and then repeated the process. He moved forward.

Well, how do you move fast like Josie did? He thought. *Oh, I guess it's just like riding a bike. Practice makes perfect!*

He stopped mid-air.

When I was play-fighting with Josie, she shot a gust of wind out of her hand. Maybe that can boost me forward! He pointed his palms behind him, focused all of his energy on his hands, and then...

KA-WOOSH!

Jets of wind shot out of his hands, propelling him forward at a fast pace. As he zoomed out of the forest, then launched into another one, he kept thinking, *Am I forgetting something?* He ignored the voice inside his head and looked down. He was over a river. It looked like there were stones ON the river, like they were made for crossing it. It looked familiar.

Then he realized, he had been here before! He was in Beachy Forest! This was the third time he had been here, yet Beachy Forest was not large. He spotted a splotch of black stu—no, Shadowstalker Ooze. THAT was where he had gotten stuck—and almost consumed. It was his first encounter with it, not counting his dream.

The forest cleared, and the ocean came into view. Ben floated down, and collapsed on the sand. He never knew flying could be so hard.

Josie, who had apparently gotten here before him, walked up to him.

"This is where you led us?" Ben complained.

"I'm surprised myself," said Josie. "This doesn't look like where Shadowstalker Ooze would be made, in the middle of the ocean."

Ben stood up, brushed himself off, and looked out to the ocean. "I don't know where the Ooze is coming from, but look. That tower over there looks weird."

"What tower?" Josie asked.

Ben pointed to a tall, thin lavender tower out in the ocean. "You know what? I think that's a mark, because this ooze is probably being made in the ocean!" he said like he'd just figured it out. "Aquamo!" He transformed into his Water Form and dived into the water.

Fast as a sailfish, he zoomed towards the tower. But as he got closer, he felt distracted, and turned around for no reason. As he drifted away from the tower, he realized his mistake and turned back toward it. But it was no use. Every time he neared the tower, he felt more and more distracted, as if everything in the world was more interesting to him than the tower. Still, he kept trying to reach it, getting closer and closer each time. Suddenly an invisible force swept over him and he passed out in the water.

CHAPTER XX

"Ben! Ben! Wake up!"

Ben opened his eyes and saw Jacob staring over him, his hands firmly clutching Ben's shoulders. He shook off his unconsciousness and sat up. "What happened?"

"You passed out in the water," Jacob explained, "but I pulled you back to shore with a vine." Ben noticed that Jacob was in his Plant Form.

Ben got up, brushed the sand off his sweatpants, and shielded his eyes with his hands.

"Where's Josie?"

"She's up there," Jacob replied, pointing to Josie, who was hovering about ten feet above the purple tower.

"How is she not being affected by the—," Ben realized he couldn't think of a word for what he was about to describe, "um— weirdness — that weird feeling— or—um..." Ben felt his cheeks getting hot.

"I know what you mean," said Jacob, "and I can explain why. I think that tower broadcasts signals—like a distracting-medicine, but only down, where it expects people to come from. The signal goes out as far as maybe twenty feet, which is why you felt it on the beach, but not upwards. So, if you somehow get directly above the tower, like Josie did, you won't feel the effects."

"I didn't get most of that, but I think I get what you mean," said Ben. He transformed into his Sky Form. He treaded air as fast as he could until he rose, and then flew over to Josie.

Jacob wrapped a vine around the tower and, like Tarzan, pulled himself to the tower.

Then he leapt on top of the tower as quickly as he could, but tripped over something.

Ben grabbed his arm and pulled him back up. "What was that?" Ben wondered.

"Look down," Jacob answered. "A hatch!" He opened the hatch and climbed down into it. Ben followed, and expected that Josie was behind--or in this case above--him.

"This is like a bottomless pit," Jacob called.

It felt like hours, but it was only a couple minutes until Ben's feet touched the cold, hard ground. "Where are we?"

Then Ben heard a deep voice below.

"Intruders! How did you get past my defenses?!"

It was a cloaked figure, and Ben couldn't see its body, just the cloak. If it was a villain, then Ben expected its voice and posture would be relaxed with a sense of authority, but it wasn't. It was practically screaming, and Ben could tell that it was NOT relaxed at all.

But Ben wasn't listening to the strange figure. Instead, he looked around. One wall was a window, gazing into the ocean. There were also three levers and some kind of control panel, but Ben didn't know what they were for. Ben never noticed Jacob was talking to the figure.

"We don't care that we're kids! We want to know what's going on here!" Jacob shouted at the figure.

Clearly Ben had missed some of the conversation.

"Too bad," said the figure. Its cloak turned icy blue in an instant.

The last thing Ben remembered hearing was KKKSSSCCCH!

CHAPTER XXI

Ben woke up feeling very cold and soaking wet. As soon as he sat up, a sharp pain seared through his head. "Ow! Brain freeze!" he cried.

But it wasn't brain freeze—Ben hadn't had a drink—or anything cold--in the last couple of hours. He was just so cold his head hurt.

He touched his shoulder next, which also felt very cold. He tried not to pay attention to the coldness and pain in his body. Ben looked around and saw large blocks of ice littered around the room. *Ice! Someone must have frozen us!* he thought.

Then he realized that being encased in ice was straight-out silly. Except...

Ben decided to think about something else. "Where am I?" he wondered out loud. It was like a large jail cell, but he didn't know where in particular.

"Shadowstalker's lair," said a voice behind him that seemed all too familiar. "I can't believe he's real either. According to *A Book of Rare and Mythological Creatures*, he's a myth. I never thought he'd actually be real!"

When Ben heard the voice mention Sadie's book by name, he realized that there was only one person he knew with that book—Sadie! Ben wondered why he had never turned around when he heard her voice. So, he did just that, and saw someone he had never expected to see again. It WAS Sadie.

"Why are YOU here?!" said both of them at the same time.

Sadie answered first. "I was just coming here to investigate that weird black stu—no, wait, it's called Shadowstalker Ooze, isn't it?"

Jacob got up, and went over to where Ben and Sadie were talking. Ben realized that he and Sadie weren't the only ones there. Jacob leaped between the two of them. "What are you DOING?" he whispered to Ben, but as loud as he could. "She's the enemy! She BETRAYED us!"

"I can still hear you," said Sadie, "and what do you mean, *I'm* the enemy? All I did was leave for a day—," she thought for a second, "—or so. Are you saying you can't survive that long without me?"

"You know very well what you did," replied Jacob. He held out his amulet, "See?!"

"I don't see anything."

"Yeah—because we healed it!" Then Jacob seemed to realize he was holding nothing in his hands. "Wait—where's my amulet?" Then he stared back at Sadie. "Well, you still crush—," Jacob paused, "—shattered our gems!"

"This is how I remember it," Sadie started. "I took your gems out and left them on the other side of the boulder, letting you fend for yourselves, about to drown, without any defense mechanism." She paused. Then she added, "Okay, I just realized how bad that sounds."

"No!" Jacob said. "You flooded Demon's Cave! You were trying to kill us! You DESTROYED our gems!"

"Wait a second," said Ben. "Maybe it WAS our fault. Maybe when we pushed back the boulder to escape, we crushed our gems ourselves..."

Ben didn't have time to finish what he was saying, because he heard a KA-CHUNK and then a VRRRR. Ben looked to his right. The jail cell was opening!

"Wait—who did that?" Ben asked.

"I did," said a voice.

CHAPTER XXII

Ben turned around. "Josie?"

"You never noticed me?" she replied.

"Who's Josie?" Sadie asked.

"We met her at the Tree of Life," Jacob replied. "But how did you get us out of here?"

"See that button?" Josie pointed to a large red button planted into the wall. "I threw my canteen through the bars and hit it, and it opened the cell."

She walked out of the jail cell and grabbed her canteen. Ben, Jacob and Sadie followed her casually.

"So... what now?" asked Ben.

"Let's just find out why we're down here," replied Jacob. "For example, what does this lever do?" He flicked a lever on the floor.

Ben heard another KA-CHUNK and VRRRR. A large metal door opened that Ben didn't see the first time he looked around because the steel door blended into the environment.

Sadie shielded her eyes, but there was absolutely no light at all in the room. "What's in here?"

Jacob clapped his hands, as if he knew how to turn on the lights in the room. The formerly pitch-black room immediately came into view.

Ben rushed to a pedestal. "Our jewelry!" He picked up each piece of jewelry and handed them to their owners.

The next thing Ben saw in the room was a glass case, with a large sphere-shaped object inside.

It was black, with a vertical rod on the top. It also looked like there was an opening.

Jacob stepped up to the case, opened it, and took out the spherical object. He studied it for a minute, and then sighed. He finally said, "I have some good news and some bad news."

"Okay," said Ben, "what's the bad news?"

"This... is a bomb."

"Yeesh!" Josie cried. "What's the good news?"

"The good news," said Jacob, "is that this is just a prototype. It can't do any real damage, because it's not stable enough."

"Well then, if you could figure that out, then what's this little capsule for?" Ben opened the tiny hatch attached to the side of the bomb. "What goes in here?"

Jacob sighed. "Okay, I'm going to try to explain this. This bomb isn't meant to inflict any damage. It's meant to spread something within a very large area—like a city. But it's NOT meant for a solid object to be put in the capsule— instead, a colloid, or a plasma, like toothpaste, for instance. So, to recap, this bomb is meant to spread something like toothpaste over a very large area. Got it?"

"Huh?" Josie said.

"Kinda," Ben replied.

Sadie seemed to understand what Jacob said. "Why would... whoever made this... want to spread a colloid throughout the city?"

"Remember, this is just a prototype," Jacob reassured her.

"Well, if there's a prototype, there has to be a product, right?" asked Sadie. "The real deal!"

Ben searched throughout the room, but he saw no bomb. "The final product isn't here."

Josie looked around the room and pointed to a glass case. "But this is! It looks exactly like the case the prototype is in, except it's empty!"

Ben got up. "Wait a second," he said, and walked over to the case Josie was standing at. He walked around to the back of the case. There was a note on the back. It read:

"Highly destructive bomb. Must fill with Shadowstalker Ooze. Set explosion for June 17th at 4:00

pm. Drop from pod as soon as possible."

Wait, Ben thought. *June 17th... that's today! And it's 3:30 right now!*

"Guys!" Ben exclaimed. "There's a bomb that's going to go off in half an hour!"

"You mean—this one? The real bomb is going off in half an hour? I don't get what you mean by that," Sadie said.

"The note says that someone filled the bomb that was in this case with Shadowstalker Ooze, and is going to drop it from a pod!"

"Wait—so they're trying to spread the city with Shadowstalker Ooze? What would they do that for?" Jacob asked.

"That's bad!" Ben said. "Shadowstalker Ooze is dangerous! It could destroy Epiconia!"

"That's probably what they were intending," said Sadie.

Josie, who had been quiet for a long time, spoke up. "We may be able to stop it, if we follow a very specific set of rules."

"Really?" Ben said, excited. "What are they?"

"We may be able to stop the Shadowstalker Ooze if we use the Life Sap as a catalyst." Josie explained. "It's like the opposite of Shadowstalker Ooze! If we stop it quickly enough, then the Life Sap can replace the ooze before it destroys everything! Plus, it's a toothpaste-sort of texture, so it can go in the prototype capsule! We will have to use all of the Life Sap we have. But we will save the world—or at least Epiconia—from destruction."

Ben thought for a moment. "That could work," he said. "But we're going to have to hurry! We don't have much time!"

Jacob had already started pouring the Life Sap from his canteen into the prototype bomb's capsule. Ben poured his in after. Once all the Life Sap from his canteen was poured, Ben concluded, "That should be enough. Josie doesn't have to use hers. And we may need it."

"Are you sure?" Josie asked.

"Keep it," Ben said.

Ben looked down at his watch. "It's 3:45," he said. "We really don't have much time! Everyone into the pods! Quick!" There were two pods behind the glass cases, they looked like cylinders with a door in the middle. It looked like there were supposed to be three, but one was already taken. One was also bigger than the other.

Josie and Jacob got into the smaller pod and shut the door. Sadie got into the larger pod. Ben grabbed the Life Sap-filled prototype bomb, and jumped into the larger pod with Sadie, who shut the door. Ben guessed the pods were intended to be emergency escape pods.

Inside the pod, there was one large window that took up most of the wall on one side. On the other side was a small control panel which included a large yellow button, and two small displays that Ben assumed showed the speed and the fuel. The gauge showed their speed as zero, because they were not moving, and the fuel gauge was halfway full. Ben pressed the large yellow button, which he assumed meant LAUNCH. He couldn't see the top of the lair, because they were in the pod, but he expected a hatch to open in the roof of the lair. He must have been correct, because soon the floor heated up and the pod blasted out of the lair.

"Okay," Sadie said, "now that we're in the pod, we need to think out our plan of action. I'll operate the controls." Ben noticed a joystick on the control panel, along with a large array of buttons, and wondered how Sadie was going to operate it.

"What do I do?" Ben asked.

"You have the most important job of all," she started.

Ben expected something silly, but she was being serious.

"You are going to drop the prototype bomb." She messed with the prototype for a second, then handed it back to Ben. "I set it to go off at 4:05. Now," she opened a small door under the control panel, and took out a machine that had two cylinders attached to each other and a remote control, "these are very important. I'll put the two cylinders onto your backpack, and you hold the remote. Once you are on top of the pod, press the first button. Once you have dropped the bomb, come back in, and I'll tell you what to do next."

Ben had one question. "How do you know all this?" he asked.

"I'll explain that later," she swiftly replied.

Ben looked out the window, and saw only blue.

Sadie inserted the two cylinders onto his backpack in a way Ben didn't understand, and opened a hatch in the top of the pod. She also pressed a button on the control panel, which made the pod stop in midair. Sadie reached up to the hatch and pulled down a ladder. "Climb up that," she said, "and remember what I told you."

Ben grabbed the rod on top of the bomb with one hand and climbed up the ladder with the other. Sadie had slipped the remote into his pants pocket.

It was very cold on top of the pod, and Ben could hardly breathe. He admired the view. He saw the forest where the Tree of Life used to be, and saw a small shape which he thought was Mt. Zekmo.

What did Sadie say? he thought. *Oh yeah! I need to press this button.* He took the remote control out of his pants pocket, but before he could press the button, he heard a loud BOOM! He looked down at the explosion.

Shadowstalker Ooze was leaking from a large crater in the ground, and fast.

He sighed. "Too late," he called to Sadie. "I guess the good side doesn't always win."

CHAPTER XXIII

"It's not too late!" Sadie called back. She pulled Ben back into the pod. "We have five more minutes before the prototype bomb goes off. At 4:04, you're going to have to go back up there and drop the prototype bomb."

"So, what should we do in these—" Ben looked down at his watch, even though he didn't have to, because he knew the product bomb would go off at four, and it was four now, "—these four minutes we have left until we drop the bomb? You know I can't stand waiting—wait a second!"

"I though you couldn't stand waiting."

"You can tell me how you know all this stuff! And why you trapped us in that cave the other day!"

Sadie hesitated, then sighed. "Fine. Okay. I trapped you in that cave because... well... you were always better at the element-stuff than me! When we were practicing on the beach, you and Jacob broke the boulder in just one shot! I broke mine in, like, five!"

Ben recalled the moment. "Two," he said.

"Whatever," she said. "The point is, you were always better at this kind of stuff than me! So—when I trapped you in Demon's Cave, I ran away to train on my own. That's when I met Shadowstalker. I didn't know who he was at the time, and he promised that if I worked for him, he would give me a shard. I was desperate. I decided to work with him. He gave me a shard, even though I thought he would break the oath and torture me or something."

Ben listened. He thought maybe he was in shock.

"I didn't," Sadie was saying, "and still don't, know what it's for, so I haven't tried it out yet. He told me his plan about setting a bomb to go off, and that's when I realized he was evil—really evil. From then on, I acted as kind of a double agent, waiting for the right moment to strike. And when I told him that I knew what he was up to, he trapped me in his prison. That's when you guys came in, and you know the rest."

Ben absorbed Sadie's story like a sponge absorbs water. "So, he told you about the pod, and how he was going to drop the bomb from the top, and all that?"

Sadie nodded. "And I wrote the note for you or Jacob to find. I wasn't sure you would trust me, but a small piece of paper started us on all this."

Ben heard a small beep.

"That's your cue," Sadie said. "It's 4:04. Try to drop the prototype bomb in the exact same place that the product bomb exploded."

"But how do I get to that place without falling off the pod?" he asked.

"I took care of that," Sadie said, and then nudged him with her elbow. "Go!"

Again, Ben climbed to the top of the pod with the bomb. He took the remote out of his pocket, and this time, had enough time to press the first button.

VOOM!

The bottoms of the two cylinders on his back heated up, and then burst into flames. The back of Ben's knees got singed, even through his sweatpants, but he ignored the mild pain as he started levitating. The cylinders were a jetpack! He flew out above the crater, and dropped the bomb.

Ben pressed the remote one last time, and the jetpack's flames stopped just over the pod. He climbed back into the pod, and Sadie swiveled the pod around so the window was facing the opposite direction it previously was. Ben could just see the prototype bomb descending.

"Three... two... one!" Sadie counted.

BOOM!

The prototype exploded in midair and gushed all the Life Sap out of it. The magical sap spread all over, feeding all the plants that got partly destroyed by the ooze. The Life Sap and the Shadowstalker Ooze merged, but the Life Sap overrode the Ooze, and stopped it in its tracks.

Ben sighed softly. "We did it," he said. "It wasn't as dramatic as I'd have hoped, but we did it."

"Don't start celebrating just yet," Sadie advised. "We still have a small problem."

"What? What is it?" Ben asked.

"We're almost all out of gas," Sadie replied somewhat casually. "But don't worry. I prepared for this." She yanked the second cylinder off Ben's jetpack easily and attached it to her own backpack. Then she climbed up the hatch, and Ben followed.

"Now what?" Ben asked.

"You still have that remote control on you?" Sadie asked.

Ben nodded, and took it out.

"Jump!" exclaimed Sadie, and before Ben had a chance to contradict her, she leaped off the top of the pod and grabbed Ben.

"Press the third button!" Sadie cried.

Ben pressed the third button on the remote control, and parachutes popped out from the cylinders attached to Ben's and Sadie's backpacks. They gently floated to the ground. Jacob's and Josie's pod gently landed, and the door opened. Jacob and Josie stepped out of the pod.

"Wow," Jacob exclaimed, "I never thought you'd actually succeed!"

"Thanks for the vote of confidence," Ben rolled his eyes.

Then a third pod landed next to Jacob's and Josie's. But whose was it?

The door dramatically opened, and out stepped a menacing figure who could only be one being: Shadowstalker.

CHAPTER XXIV

Well, this is unexpected. Ben couldn't see under the dark cloak, but he could tell that Shadowstalker was enraged. "You—you BEAT my UNBEATABLE plan!"

Jacob seemed way too confident. "I don't think it's unbeatable anymore, 'cause we just beat it."

Shadowstalker seemed to ignore Jacob, and as quick as lightning, he shot a flurry of punches at Ben, so quick that Ben couldn't see his fists—if he had fists.

Ben slid to the left, and then ran as fast as he could towards a huge slope beneath a cliff. Ben was cornered.

Shadowstalker quickly shot an enormous black blast out of his cloak to finish off Ben. "You may have defeated my plan, but you will not defeat me!"

Before he had time to think, a flaming shield surrounded Ben. And in less than a second, the black blast surrounded the shield, and exploded, somehow leaving the shield unharmed. The shield then flickered and disappeared. Had he had transformed into his Fire Form? Ben didn't know.

Ben ran out towards the open, but Shadowstalker shot another incredibly large black blast at him. This blast was much larger than the first.

His instincts took over and Ben shot a jet of fire out of his hands, though not as nearly as big as Shadowstalker's blast.

The two blasts met, but Shadowstalker's looked like it was going to overpower Ben's blast with ease.

"A little help here?" Ben shivered in fear.

Jacob transformed into his Electric Form and blasted a lightning bolt out of his hands toward Shadowstalker's blast. "Don't worry," he said, "I got your back."

"Me too!" exclaimed Josie as she transformed into her Sky Form and a huge gust of wind exploded from her hands.

"And me...I guess," Sadie transformed into her Water Form and a huge jet of water blasted out of her palms.

It looked like the four blasts were going to overpower Shadowstalker's, but the evil being still hung on.

Ben was pushing as hard as he could. "Push your blasts as hard as you can!" he told Jacob, Sadie, and Josie.

"We are!" they said in unison.

"We just need an extra boost to push us over the edge!" Ben cried.

Suddenly and unexpectedly, three small figures leapt out of the bushes and jumped next to Sadie. One of them shot fire, one of them water, and one of them lightning, from what seemed to be their mouths. This was the extra push that they needed to overpower Shadowstalker.

They heard an earsplitting screech, and a flash of blinding light, and Shadowstalker was gone. All that was left was a small, black, metal ring.

Sadie snagged the ring, trying to act like no nobody saw, even though Ben did.

Ben, Jacob, and Josie looked down at the three small things that saved them from Shadowstalker's wrath. They immediately recognized them.

Josie spoke first. "Bolt! Magma! But... who's this other dragon?"

Before anyone could answer, Ben and Jacob scooped up each of their dragons. "We're so glad Josie put you someplace safe while we fought that bad guy! Look how big you've gotten!" they cried.

Josie blushed, though nobody noticed.

Sadie looked at the other dragon. It was blue with purple stripes and quite a bit smaller than Bolt and Magma. "This must be mine," she said. "I must have left my egg in a bush or something while I was talking to Shadowstalker, and then it hatched." She silenced Jacob and Josie before they started asking questions. "Long story," she said, and then, "Why is she so small?"

Josie replied, "I'm going to have to introduce you to the Tree of Life Sap."

Jacob looked up at the sky; the sun was quite close to setting. "Well," he said to Josie, "we should head home."

Why, Ben thought sarcastically, *we've been on this massive adventure for two days.*

Josie sighed. "I'll go home too," she said. But as the four adventurers, and the three dragons, headed to their respective homes, they followed the same path.

"Are you following me?" said Josie.

"It looks like you're following us," Ben replied.

After a while, Josie said, "Do you feel like we're being watched?" Ben turned and saw two shining red eyes starting at him through the bushes, which quickly disappeared.

"Guys, seriously, I think the Natig—" Ben began.

"Well, this is our neighborhood," Sadie announced.

But as they neared their houses, they discovered something.

"Wait, this is my neighborhood too!" Josie exclaimed. "We live near each other!"

As soon as they found out this fact, they settled in the shade of a nearby oak tree. While the sun was setting, they shared stories about their recent adventures, and they were sure they would come across a new one together another day. But for now, they relaxed, and enjoyed being there. There were a lot of loose ends, but everyone knew they would tie them up someday.

Acknowledgements

To YCDS class of 2025, and everyone who will follow them and that came before them.

To Phyl Campbell, who taught me, and

To my parents, who brought me to the amazing classes where I learned so much!